Lighthouse Fireflies

Written by Anne Margaret Lewis
Illustrated by Mary Frey

Mackinac Island Press

for the love of reading

First Edition

Library of Congress Cataloging-in-Publication Data

Lewis, Anne Margaret and Frey, Mary
Lighthouse Fireflies
Summary: Lighthouse Fireflies takes you on a whirlwind adventure when a lighthouse keeper's son catches King Firefly and must release him.
ISBN 0-9749145-4-1
Fiction

10 9 8 7 6 5 4 3 2 1

Printed and bound in Canada by Friesens, Altona, Manitoba.

A Mackinac Island Press, Inc. publication
www.mackinacislandpress.com

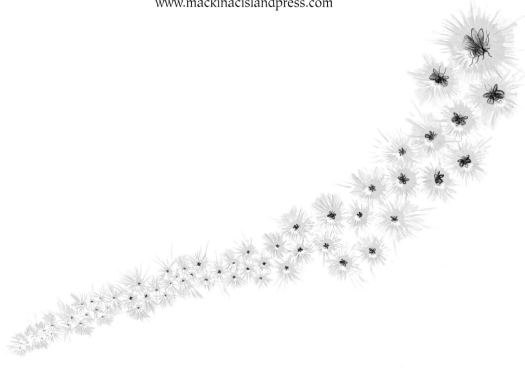

We lived in the lighthouse at the end of the beach.
It needed repair and the roof often leaked.
Dad was the loyal lighthouse keeper.
Me? I was the wee little lighthouse sweeper.

It was a hot, muggy summer night.
The sun had just set in time for the fireflies' flight.
It was the fireflies' turn to light up the night sky,
flickering about like fireflies fly.

I opened my jar hoping one would fly in,
the bottom made from glass and the top made from tin.
I decided to be as quiet as a mouse scurrying in the sand,
silently setting my jar down to catch a firefly by hand.

When I peeked through my thumbs I could see a light blinking.
I slid him into the jar...he began clanking and clinking.
Mom called me inside: "It's time to go to bed!"
I looked at my new friend. "I'll take care of you," I said.

My shiny new nightlight made me feel safe,
like the boats in the harbor when coming in late.

I noticed something different about this firefly—
he was bigger than the others. "Hmmm," I wondered,
"Why?"
His light shone brighter and longer than the rest.
I looked through the glass and whispered, "You're the best."

The next morning when I woke up,
I looked over at my new little light.
Firefly looked sad...I wondered if he was all right.
He was flicking on the glass to the beat of S-O-S.
"Help...let me out!" he seemed to request.

As I was cleaning the fireplace, cinders started to fly.
I noticed a yellow glow out of the corner of my eye.
"Psst! Psst!" I heard, coming from the window sill.
"Over here!" cried a firefly, with a high-pitched shrill.

"Hey you…little lighthouse sweeper," he peeped.
"You've got King Firefly." Then he started to leap
toward my head; he was angrily flying
and buzzing around me, wildly crying.

"You have the king of the fireflies,
who leads us to safety.
I beg you, lighthouse sweeper, please set him free!"
"What would you do if your lighthouse
light broke down?"
"How would you guide the boats safely to town?"

"I know his sparkling glow makes you feel safe at night.
If you must have a firefly, take me… I'm almost as bright."

"Calm down, little firefly," I said with a sigh.
"Just give me a moment to say thanks and goodbye!"

"There's no time to spare, little lighthouse sweeper!" he said with a yelp.
"There's a storm coming in, and the fireflies need the King's help!"

"He must lead us to safety, back to our firefly home,
the floor made of sand and the walls made from stone.
King Firefly has the brightest firefly light
to keep all of his firefly friends close in his sight."

I released King Firefly into the wind,
watching the stormy waters with the boats coming in.
King Firefly was free with his light shining bright,
but the lighthouse was not, on this dark stormy night.
Off to the lighthouse so quickly I ran,
to help the lighthouse keeper...I know that I can!

Lightning was dancing all over the place.
I could see the worry on Dad's rugged face.

Dad said, "I've got bad news, my son.
The lighthouse light is finally done.
The equipment is too old and the signal won't blink."
"There has to be a way to save the boats," and I started to think....

"Hmmm…what would you do if your lighthouse light broke down?"
"How would you guide the boats safely to town?"

I remembered what the firefly had said.
Just then I felt something land on my head.

As he started to fly around my head in a ring,
I realized it was the one and only...the Firefly King!
"You answered my SOS and were loyal to me.
I'm here to return the favor, you see."

I watched as he headed toward the lighthouse stairs all a twinkle.
He stopped for a moment and let out his S-O-S signal.
Then, in by the thousands came all of his firefly friends,
twirling up the lighthouse steps, to the top they would tend.

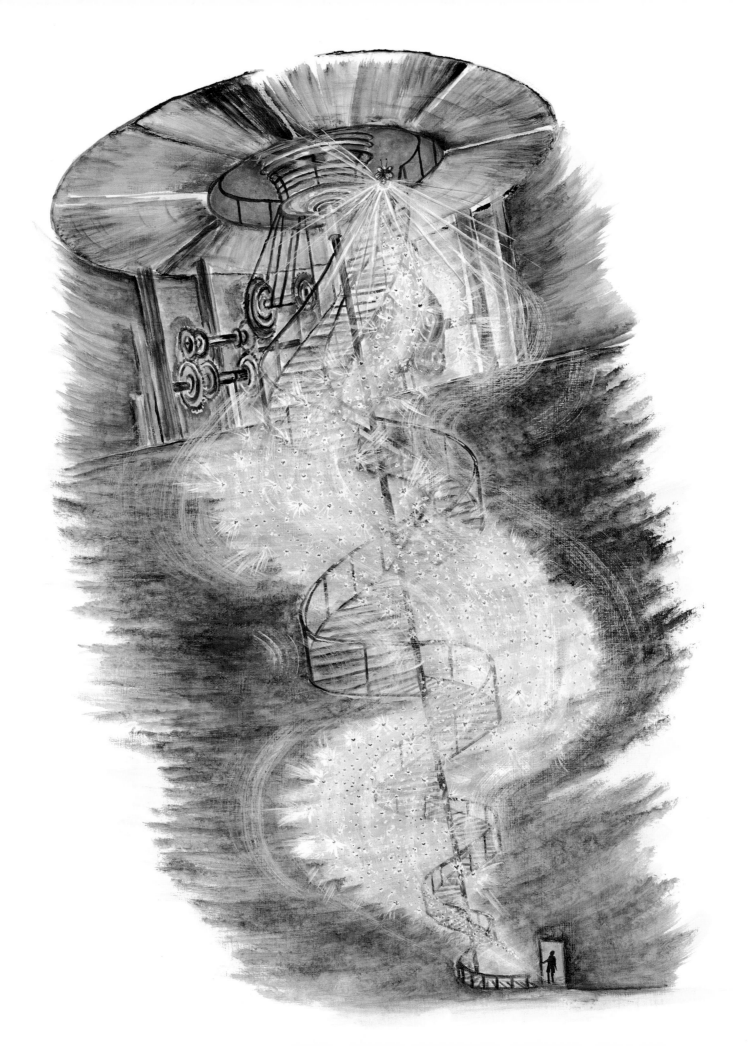

They sent the lighthouse signal all through the storm.
It was at that very moment that lighthouse fireflies were born.

I said gratefully, "Thank you, King Firefly
and all of your friends."
King Firefly and lighthouse sweeper were friends forever....
THE END.